When you are sorrowful, look again in your heart,
and you shall see that in truth you are weeping
for that which has been your delight.

The Prophet

for Kathy & Cherry

Copyright © 1991 by Rachel Pank.
All rights reserved. Published by Scholastic Inc.,
by arrangement with ABC, All Books for Children,
a division of The All Children's Company Ltd.,
33 Museum Street, London WC1A 1LD, England.

SCHOLASTIC HARDCOVER is a registered trademark of Scholastic Inc.

Library of Congress Cataloging-in-Publication Data
Pank, Rachel.
Under the blackberries / by Rachel Pank.
p.   cm.
Summary: Sonia and her cat Barnie are inseparable, until
the day there is an accident and he goes away for good.
ISBN 0-590-45481-1
[1. Cats—Fiction.] I. Title.
PZ7.P18935Un 1992
[E]—dc20   91-19669
                                                        CIP
                                                        AC
12 11 10 9 8 7 6 5 4 3 2 1   2 3 4 5 6/9
Printed in Hong Kong.
First Scholastic printing, May 1992

Under the Blackberries

Rachel Pank

SCHOLASTIC
HARDCOVER

Scholastic Inc. · New York

Sonia and Barnie went everywhere together.

Down the garden, up the garden,
up the stairs, down the stairs.
When Sonia took things out of her
cupboard, Barnie got *in* her cupboard.

When Sonia got out of her bath and emptied it,
Barnie got in and drank a few drops from the drain.
(Of course, Mom insisted that Barnie drink from his bowl,
so every day Sonia would fill it up, then whisper to him,
"It's OK, you can drink from the drain later.")

The garden was the best place for Barnie. Sonia knew all his hiding places and where to look if he didn't come in for his dinner. Barnie would wait for ages, then come running out of his little, flattened nest under the blackberry bushes between the roses where he had been snoozing, and pretend that, really, he had been on an exciting, hunting expedition.

In winter Barnie always slept on
Sonia's bed. When it was really
cold, he tried to burrow under
the covers like a mole until
he reached her feet.

In summer he crept from one shady
place in the garden to another, and
only slunk into the sun for
a lick of Sonia's ice cream
or to chase a fly.

Sonia had never thought that Barnie wouldn't be there to follow her. But one morning—he wasn't. No, he wasn't. She ran through the house. She looked in the cupboards and under the beds. No, he definitely wasn't there.

"But Barnie's always there," Sonia thought as she ran into the garden. "I mean, he just is," she said to Jasper, the-cat-next-door, who came with her to look under the blackberries.

"Where is he, Jasper?" she asked very seriously, looking him in the eyes.

Jasper looked back. He didn't know. Sonia sat down in the long grass and cried. Jasper sat nearby, which was very nice of him, because cats don't usually like hearing people cry.

Sadly, the day didn't get better. "You see,"
Sonia later explained to Jasper, who was sitting in
the afternoon sun, "Dad says Barnie ran into the
road and there was an accident and . . ." Sonia
was very brave. "He's dead," she whispered.

She had to whisper because she was afraid
that saying it out loud would make it true.

But it was true, and there was nothing Sonia could do
to make Barnie come back, so she cried a lot. Mom made
her a special snack. Dad let her play Grandad's musical box
and then they all squashed together on the sofa. Sonia
cried again and baby Sam cried, too, because he didn't
like having a sister with a red nose and puffy eyes.

Later Sonia was allowed
to have a last look in the garden.
"Well, he might just be out there,"
she said. "He might just be hiding."
But he didn't seem to be. Just in case,
Sonia left a saucer of milk and some
cookies out for him. "He might
just be hungry," she said.

Sonia put all the toys she could
find in her bed before she climbed in.
There wasn't much room and they were
lumpy and bumpy and Sonia felt cross with
them, because they weren't Barnie.

It was no good, and in the end she had
two chocolate cookies and some milk and
then got into Mom and Dad's bed.

She woke up early and went into the garden. A porcupine was drinking the milk, so in a way Sonia was glad she'd left it there. But she didn't know what to do now, because nothing was the same without Barnie.

"Nothing seems right," Sonia cried to the porcupine, who stayed close by. This was nice of the porcupine, because they don't like people crying much either. Sonia decided this was a sign of a good friend and she went to get the porcupine another drink.

In the afternoon, Dad dug a hole
in the exact place where Sonia pointed.
"No, not there . . . no, not there." She waved her arms.
"Nearly, no, this way a bit," she instructed him. This
was where Barnie would be buried. Sonia invited the
neighbors and her best friends, Kathy and Cherry, who
had cried, too, when she told them about Barnie.

Mom found a box that was just the right size and
special enough for poor Barnie. Sonia tied the box up
with her favorite pink hair ribbon. It was very sad, but
everyone kissed her and said what a lovely cat
Barnie was. Even the neighbor seemed to
forget about the time Barnie had
dug a hole in her herb garden.

Kathy and Cherry helped Sonia cover the grave with
rose petals. "We're going to plant a rosebush here,"
Sonia said, "and I'll be the one who waters it."

Sonia had her snack with Kathy and Cherry on the grass so they could be near to the spot where Barnie was buried, and they fed Jasper bits of ham (when Mom wasn't looking).

A few weeks later, even though she still cried now and then, Sonia didn't feel *quite* so sad. She played with Jasper and fed the porcupine and telephoned her friends a lot.

"Sometimes I almost think I see Barnie in the shady parts of the bushes," she said to Kathy on the phone. "It's not scary, it's nice, like he's still here—even though he isn't."

"He's special," agreed Kathy, "like my rabbit, Rupert."

That evening, Mom and Dad were very excited. They led Sonia into the living room with her eyes closed. When she opened them, she saw a cat basket. There were little scratching sounds coming from inside!

"It's a kitten for you," Dad said. Sonia felt a bit strange having a cat that wasn't Barnie. She took the kitten out of the basket and held it close.

She felt its little heart beating fast. "Mew," said the kitten, "mew, mew!" Sonia knew that she loved the kitten and that the kitten loved her.

"She's called Daisy!" said Sonia and went to find
her softest, fluffiest sweater for Daisy to sleep on.

Soon Daisy was big enough to play in the garden. She was still young and silly though, and kept rushing up and down and then standing still with her head to one side. It took a long time to teach her not to climb on Barnie's special rosebush. Daisy did try hard to remember, but sometimes she forgot. When she did forget, Jasper would remind her by rolling her over with his big orange paw.

Sonia would smile. "All the rest of the garden is for you, but this place is special, because it's for Barnie and for me, and that will never change."